Little Rabbits' First Farm Book

Note to Parents

All pre-school children love looking at animals, imitating their sounds and learning about their homes and routines, so this book will provide hours of fun. The playful story and irresistible cast of farmyard animals will delight the very youngest child, whilst older children will be fascinated by the abundant detail on every page.

This book offers a wealth of early learning experiences. Talk about the story to develop your child's vocabulary and encourage verbal fluency. Draw attention to familiar words to instil confidence with the idea of printed language. Discuss the details in the pictures to develop observational skills – which will be important later for learning to read – and play the games at the end of the book to reinforce these skills and introduce new ones.

Little Rabbits' First Farm Book also offers an excellent way to introduce your child to life beyond the home and broaden their experience of the outside world. In our increasingly urban society it is more important than ever to appreciate how nature affects our everyday lives, since by understanding our environment we can protect it. Discovering how animals are reared and how food is grown will help your child to develop an affinity with the natural world and an interest in preserving it for the future. Above all, learning about the farm is fun – so delight in your child's excitement as they find out more about the world around them.

The Publisher wishes to thank Jill Clay, Education Consultant to the National Union of Farners, for her kind assistance in the development of this book.

KINGFISHER
An imprint of Kingfisher Publications Plc
New Penderel House, 283-288 High Holborn
London WC1V 7HZ

First published in hardback by Kingfisher 2001
First published in paperback by Kingfisher 2003
2 4 6 8 10 9 7 5 3 1
ITR/1102/TWP/FR/150SEM

Text and illustrations copyright © Alan Baker 2001

The moral right of the author has been asserted.

A CIP catalogue record for this book is available from the British Library.

ISBN 0 7534 0830 9

Printed in Singapore

Little Rabbits'
First Farm Book

Alan Baker

KINGFISHER

Wake up, farm!

It's early in the morning and the Little Rabbits
have come to help on the farm.
The cockerel is crowing.

Cock-a-doodle-doo!

Time for all the animals to wake up!

Chickens clucking

The hens and the chicks are first to be fed.
Black and White Rabbit gives them corn to eat.
Grey Rabbit collects the eggs from the hen house.

Did You Know?

Hens can lay eggs every day.
Look what eggs are used for:

Animal Families

Cockerel

Hen

Chick

Ducks quacking

Brown Rabbit is feeding the ducks.
The fluffy ducklings are swimming in the pond.
Don't fall in the water, Brown Rabbit!

Quack!
Quack!

Did You Know?
Ducks have webbed feet to help them swim.

Animal Families

Drake

Duck

Duckling

11

Cattle moo-ing

The bull and the cow are ready for breakfast.
Here comes Grey Rabbit with some hay for them.
Look who is feeding the new calf!

Moo! Moo!

Did You Know?

Cows eat grass to make milk. Hay is dried grass.

Milk comes out of the cow's udder.

Animal Families

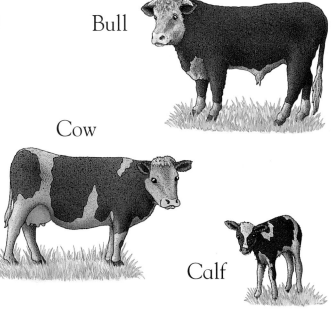

Bull

Cow

Calf

Pigs oinking

The pigs and the piglets are hungry, too.
White Rabbit pours grain into the trough.
The piglets snuggle up to drink their milk.

Oink!
Oink!

Did You Know?

Pigs live in sties. They love to roll around in the mud. Mud protects them from the sun.

Animal Families

Boar

Sow

Piglet

Sheep baa-ing

Brown Rabbit is taking the sheep to a field where there is lots of juicy fresh grass to eat. Hurry up, little lambs!

Baa! Baa!

Did You Know?

Sheep have a woolly coat to keep them warm. Look what else wool is used for:

Animal Families

Ram

Ewe

Lamb

Tractor chugging

It's time to plant the seeds that will grow into wheat.
White Rabbit drives the tractor across the field.
What a lot of noise it makes!

Chug!
Chug!
Chug!

Did You Know?

Tractors pull machines called ploughs to dig up the ground and make it ready for planting.

Wheat gives us grain, which is made into flour.

FLOUR

Look what flour is used for:

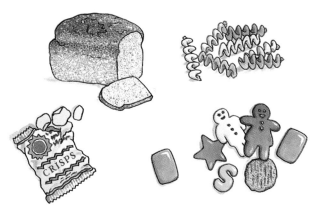

Picking the apples

The apples in the orchard are ready for picking. Some are growing right at the top of the trees. Hold on tight, Black and White Rabbit!

Did You Know?

Lots of different fruits and vegetables are grown on the farm.

Look what apples are used for:

Milking the cows

Now it's time for the cows to be milked.
Brown Rabbit collects the milk in a pail.
Mind the swishy tail, White Rabbit!

Did You Know?

Cows are milked twice a day on the farm. Most are milked by a special machine.

A tanker takes the milk to the factory.

Look what milk is used for:

Let's go shopping

The farm shop sells food that comes from the farm. Black and White Rabbit has a long shopping list. What do you want for dinner, Little Rabbits?

Did You Know?

Most food produced on the farm is taken away by trucks to be sold.

BUNNY'S BEST   FARM FOODS

Look where food is sold:

BUNNY GROCERY

FRUIT & VEG

SUPERMARKET

Goodnight, farm

It's late now and the Little Rabbits must go home.
Don't forget to shut the gate behind you!

Zzzz, zzzz!

Goodnight, farm.
Goodnight, Little Rabbits.

Games to play

Playing these games with your child will help them to develop observational, verbal and sorting skills. You will be building their understanding of the world around them and providing the foundation for early literacy and numeracy.

Names and noises

Children love identifying animals and imitating their sounds. Pointing to the pictures, ask your child to name each animal and to make the right animal sound. Alternatively, ask your child to point to the animal whose sound you make. Match the picture of each animal to its label to encourage recognition of these familiar word

Mix and match

Does the cow live in the hen house? Does the pig live in the pond? Help your child to match each animal to its farmyard home.

All different kinds

Looking at colour, shape and pattern, help your child describe how the farm animals differ from one anothe – and in which ways they are similar. How many animals have two legs and how many have four? Extend and practise vocabulary by providing further detail with words such as fur, feathers, fleece and tail.

Where's Mouse?

Children adore the game of hide-and-seek. Ask your child to find the little brown mouse that appears throughout the book and help your child to describe what he is doing.

Food on the farm

Look at the food you have at home and talk to your child about how this came to be there. Which of the foods described in the book can they find in their refrigerator or store cupboard? You may decide to extend this to a discussion about foods not mentioned in the book but familiar to your own child – for example, animal products such as meat.

Day and night on the farm

Try this simple game of spot the difference. Look again at the opening pages 6 and 7 and the closing pages 26 and 27. What differences can your child identify between the two scenes? Use this as a basis for a discussion about time – day and night and early and late – and the routines associated with different times of the day.

Animals everywhere

Match up the words to the pictures.

boar
bull
calf
chick
cockerel
cow
drake
duck
duckling
ewe
hen
lamb
piglet
ram
sow

Now match the baby animals to their parents.

Collect all the Little Rabbit books by Alan Baker!

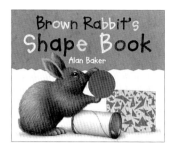

Brown Rabbit's
Shape Book

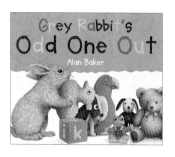

Grey Rabbit's
Odd One Out

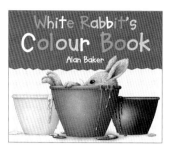

White Rabbit's
Colour Book

Black and White Rabbit's
ABC

Little Rabbits'
First Number Book

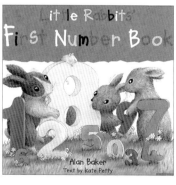

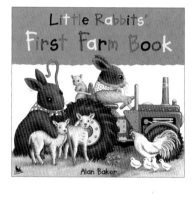

Little Rabbits'
First Farm Book

Little Rabbits'
Tell the Time Book

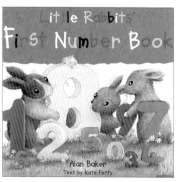

Little Rabbits'
Picture Word Book

BRILLIANT

To Ann-Janine, Caroline and Suzanne – with thanks from Tony.
For Mister Mush and Scampy – A.P.

The Publisher thanks the National Maritime Museum, Greenwich for
their kind assistance in the development of this book.

KINGFISHER
An imprint of Kingfisher Publications Plc
New Penderel House, 283-288 High Holborn, London WC1V 7HZ
www.kingfisherpub.com

First published by Kingfisher 2002
This edition first published by Kingfisher 2007
2 4 6 8 10 9 7 5 3 1

A CIP catalogue record for this book is available from the British Library.

ISBN: 978 0 7534 1521 4

Printed in China
1TR/0707/WKT/CG(SCHOY)/157MA/C

BRILLIANT BOATS

Tony Mitton and
Ant Parker

KINGFISHER

Boats are really brilliant for sailing us around.
They travel through the water
with a sloppy-slappy sound.

It's fun to go out boating, especially in the sun.
The water's cool and sparkly,
so come on everyone!

A boat sits on the water
like an empty bowl or cup.
It's hollow and it's full of air,
and that's what keeps it up.

An anchor holds you steady
when you're bobbing in a bay.
You wind a chain to raise it
when you want to sail away.

Over lakes and seas and rivers,
wind blows very strong.
Some boats have sails to catch it,
so it pushes them along.

To manage boats with masts and sails,
you need a clever crew.
The captain is the one in charge,
who tells them what to do.

A dinghy or a rowing boat
is useful near the shore.

You make it travel backwards
by pulling on each oar.

Whoosh!

A motor boat is powered
by propeller from the back.
It whooshes through the water
and leaves a foamy track.

And just in case, by accident,
you tumble from the boat,
you have to wear a life jacket,
made to help you float.

Some boats go out fishing
where the ocean waves are steep.

Their nets are cast to catch the fish,
then haul them from the deep.

A ship can carry cargo,
which is loaded at the docks.

Hup! Ho! Look out below!
Here comes a giant box.

A ferry carries cars and lorries
where they need to go.

The people travel up above.
The vehicles stay below.

A mighty ocean liner
has a big and busy crew.
It carries many passengers.
They're waving now. Yoo-hoo!

The ship has cosy cabins
where the passengers can stay.
And out on deck they stroll about
and watch the sea, or play.

But when the journey's over –
Ahoy! The lighthouse rock!

The ship glides into harbour
and ties up at the dock.

Boat bits

lighthouse

this is a tall building on the coast with a flashing light to guide ships and keep them away from rocks

anchor

this is a very heavy piece of metal with hooks which dig into the ground under the water to stop the boat drifting away

propeller

this has **blades** which spin round very fast at the back of the boat and push against the water to move the boat forward

oars

these are long poles with flat **blades** at the end which push against the water to move the boat forward

deck

this is the floor of a boat

cabin

this is the little room where you sleep on board a boat

cargo

this is the name for the goods that a ship transports

MANDY

← name

many boats are given names by their owners

FRAGILE